My Father Knows the Names of Things

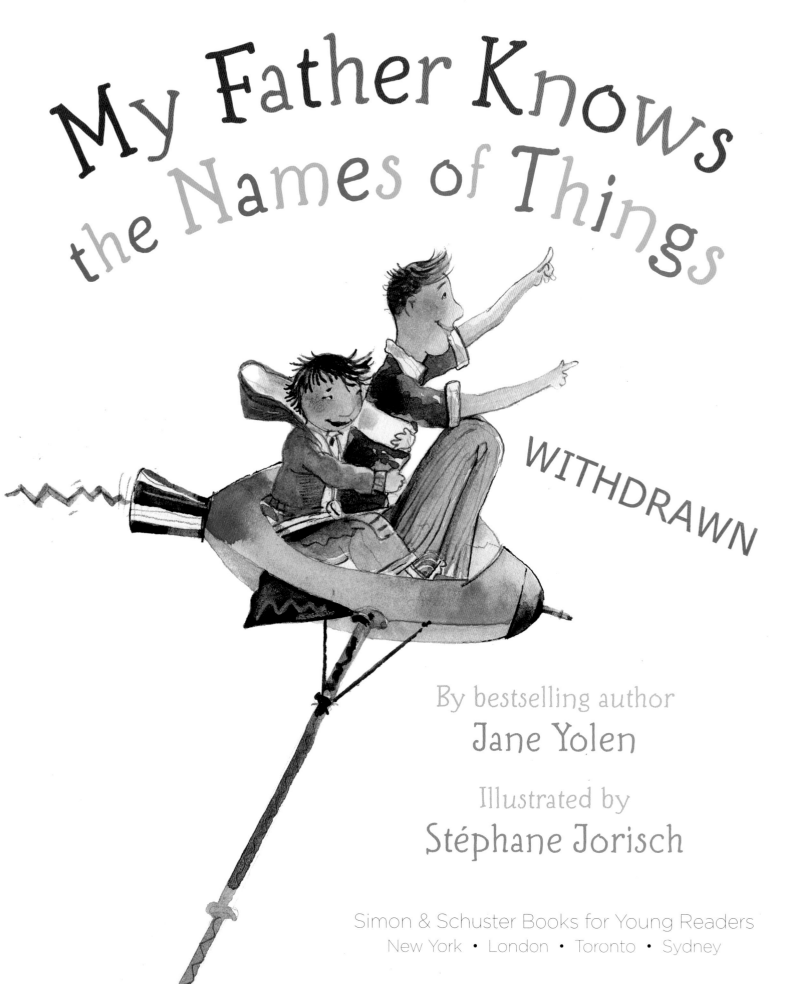

By bestselling author
Jane Yolen

Illustrated by
Stéphane Jorisch

Simon & Schuster Books for Young Readers
New York • London • Toronto • Sydney

SIMON & SCHUSTER BOOKS FOR YOUNG READERS
An imprint of Simon & Schuster Children's Publishing Division
1230 Avenue of the Americas, New York, New York 10020
Text copyright © 2010 by Jane Yolen
Illustrations copyright © 2010 by Stéphane Jorisch
SIMON & SCHUSTER BOOKS FOR YOUNG READERS is a trademark of Simon & Schuster, Inc.
Book design by Lizzy Bromley
The text for this book is set in Alghera.
The illustrations for this book are rendered in watercolor, gouache, pen, and ink.
Manufactured in China
2 4 6 8 10 9 7 5 3 1
Library of Congress Cataloging-in-Publication Data
Yolen, Jane.
My father knows the names of things / Jane Yolen ; illustrated by Stéphane Jorisch.
p. cm.
ISBN: 978-1-4169-4895-7 (hardcover)
[1. Stories in rhyme. 2. Father and child—Fiction. 3. Names—Fiction.] I. Jorisch, Stéphane, ill. II. Title.
PZ8.3.Y76My 2010
[E]—dc22
2007041840

first
edition

In memory of David Stemple,
"The Man Who Knew Everything,"
father to Heidi, Adam, and Jason,
who learned so much from his
awesome knowledge and fierce curiosity:
birds and birdsong especially.
—J. Y.

To the little boys in dads
—S. J.

My father knows the names of things,
Each bird that sings,
Their nicknames, too,

He knows the names of dogs

And cheese

And seven words that all mean blue.

He knows which mosses are the fuzziest,

He knows which insects are the buzziest,

And when we're sailing on the sea
He tells the names of fish to me.

My father knows the names of things,
Each different sort of bell that rings,
And stones,

And knows the names of planets,
Stars,

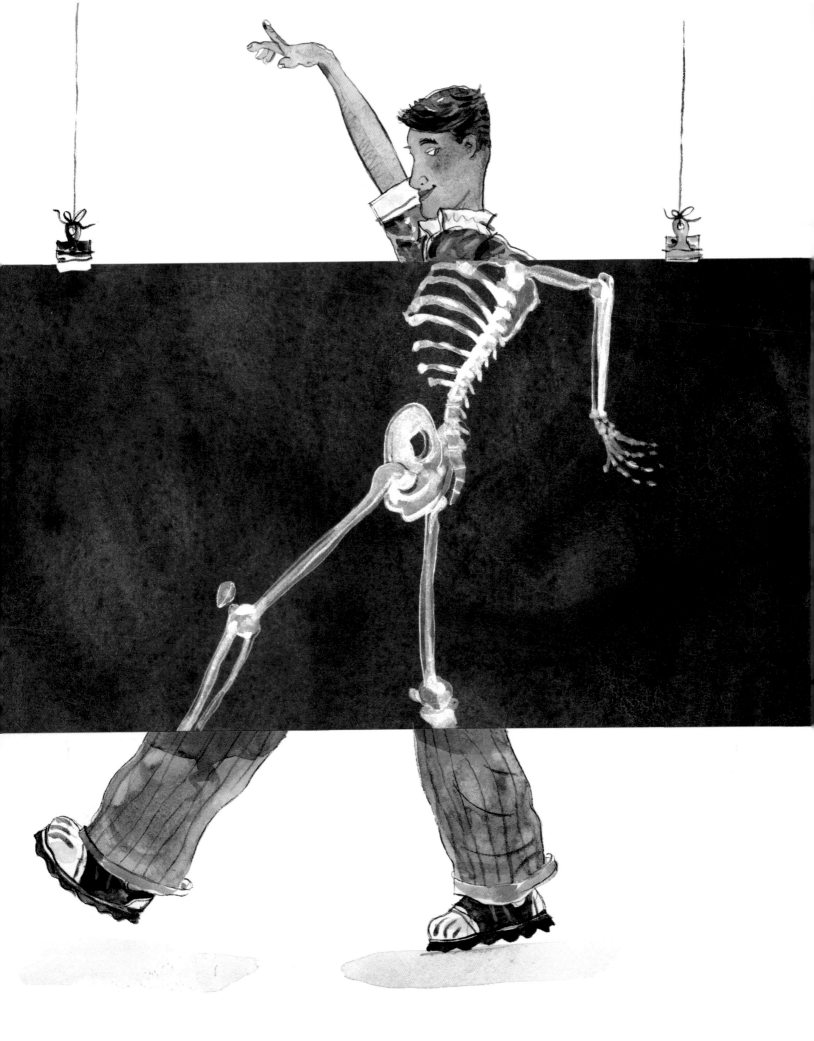

And even human bones.

He knows which flowers are the tallest,

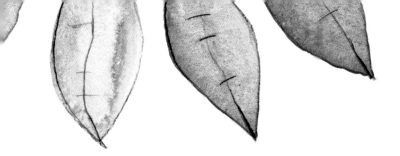

And which beetles are the smallest,

And when we fly, he says out loud
The name of every kind of cloud.

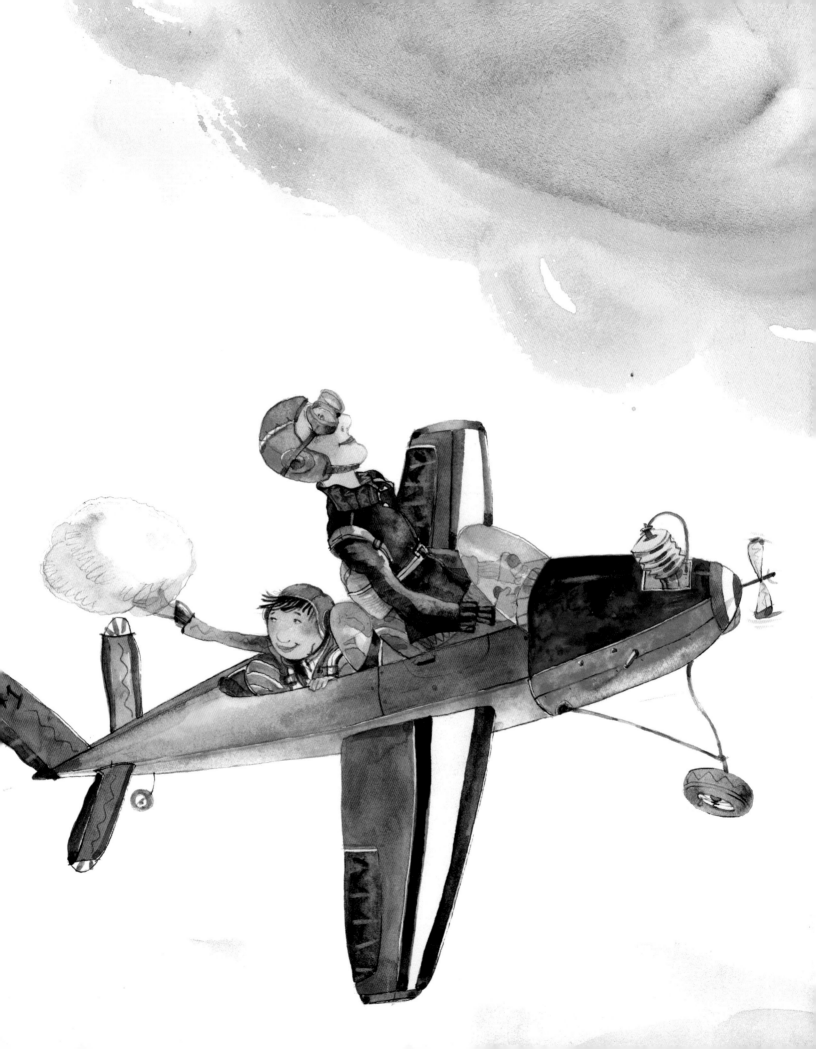

My father knows the names of things,
Of every kind of bug that stings,
And bites.

He knows the names of cats

And candies

And a dozen other words for night.

He knows which dinosaurs are meanest,

He knows which soaps can make you cleanest,

He points out everything we see
And teaches all the names to me.